青蛙和蟾蜍
好伙伴
Frog and Toad Together

文／圖　艾諾・洛貝爾 *Arnold Lobel*

譯　潘人木　黨英台

我會讀系列 中英雙語

○上誼

Frog and Toad Together (bilingual edition)

Copyright © 1971,1972 by Arnold Lobel

Published by arrangement with Harper & Row, Publishers, Inc.,

New York, N. Y., U. S. A.

Chinese Text © HSINEX INTERNATIONAL CORPORATION 1989

中文版授權 上誼文化實業股份有限公司

青蛙和蟾蜍———好伙伴（中英雙語）

文、圖／艾諾・洛貝爾　譯／黨英台　譯文審定者／潘人木

總策畫／張杏如　總編輯／高明美　企劃／溫碧珠、邱孟嫻

執行編輯／郭恩惠　美術編輯／廖瑞文、林勵勳　生產管理／王彥森

發行人／張杏如　出版／上誼文化實業股份有限公司　地址／台北市重慶南路二段75號

電話／(02)23913384(代表號)　網址／http://www.hsin-yi.org.tw

郵撥／10424361　上誼文化實業股份有限公司　定價／(書＋英文 CD)220 元

2001年6月初版　2014年1月初版十四刷　ISBN／957-762-245-3

印刷／中華彩色印刷股份有限公司

有版權・勿翻印　如有破損或裝訂錯誤請寄回更換　　讀者服務／信誼・奇蜜親子網 www.kimy.com.tw

目　次

Contents

工作表

一天早晨，
蟾蜍坐在床上，
他說：
「我有好多事情要做，
我要把所有的事情
一件一件寫下來，
列一張表，
才不會忘記。」
他找出一張紙，
在上面寫：
今天要做的事
然後他寫
起床

4

寫完了，他說：

「這件事我已經做了。」

他就畫掉了：

~~起床~~

5

然後蟾蜍繼續在那張紙上寫：

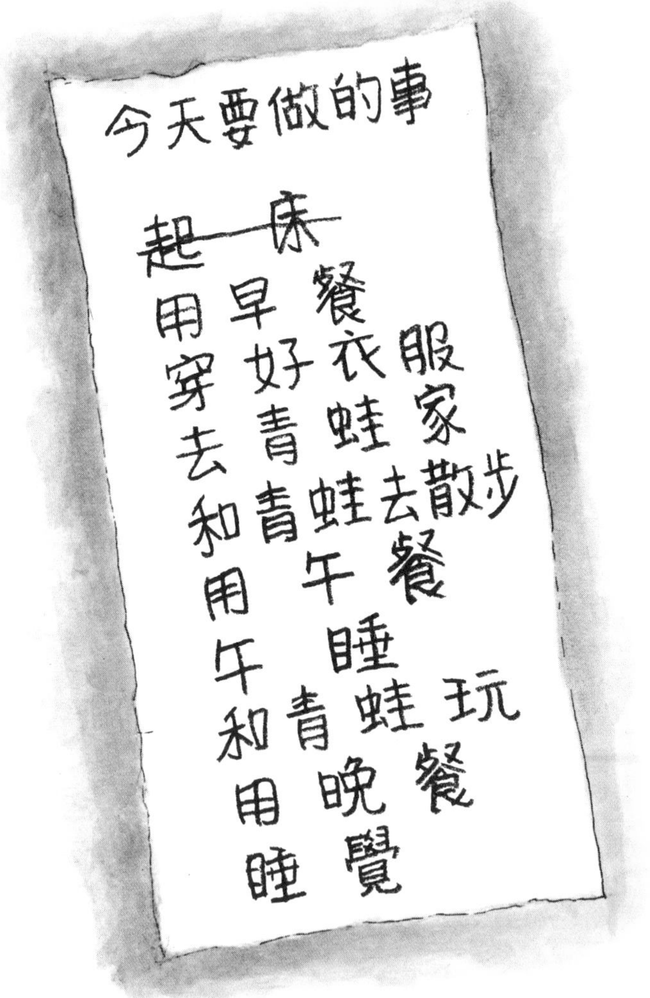

今天要做的事

起床
用早餐
穿好衣服
去青蛙家
和青蛙去散步
用午餐
午睡
和青蛙玩
用晚餐
睡覺

「這下好了，」
蟾蜍說：
「我一天該做的事情
全寫下來了。」
他下了床，
吃點東西。
然後他畫掉了：

~~用早餐~~

蟾蜍從衣櫥裡

拿出幾件衣服

穿在身上。

然後畫掉了

~~穿好衣服~~

蟾蜍把這張表

放進口袋裡。

他開了門走出去，
走進清新的晨光中。
不一會兒，
蟾蜍就到了青蛙的門口。
他從口袋裡掏出那張表，
畫掉了：

去青蛙家

9

蟾蜍敲敲門。

青蛙開門出來，說：

「嗨！」

蟾蜍說：「你來看看，

這是我今天的工作表。」

「嗯，很好。」青蛙說。

蟾蜍立刻說：

「按照我這張表，

現在我們應該去散步。」

「好啊，」青蛙說：

「我準備好了，走吧。」

10

青蛙和蟾蜍

走了很長一段路。

然後蟾蜍又從他的

口袋裡掏出那張表，

他畫掉了：

~~和青蛙去散步~~

這時候，

恰巧吹來一陣大風，

把蟾蜍手上的工作表

吹走了，

一直吹到高高的空中。

「救命啊！」蟾蜍大叫：

「我的工作表被吹跑了，

12

沒ㄇㄟˊ有ㄧㄡˇ它ㄊㄚ，
我ㄨㄛˇ怎ㄗㄣˇ麼˙ㄇㄜ辦ㄅㄢˋ事ㄕˋ呢˙ㄋㄜ？」

13

青蛙說：「趕快！
我們跑去追啊，
把它給抓回來。」
「不行，」蟾蜍說：
「我不能去追。」
「為什麼？」青蛙問。
「因為，」
蟾蜍哭喪著臉說：
「我的工作表上
並沒有列出
追工作表這一條啊！」

14

青蛙跑去追那張表。
他越過小山，
穿過沼澤，
可是那張工作表
被吹得越來越遠。
最後青蛙只好回到
蟾蜍身邊。
「對不起，」青蛙跑得
上氣不接下氣的說：
「我沒有追到
你的工作表。」
「真倒霉，」
蟾蜍說：

「 工作表上寫的工作
我是一樣也記不得，
我只好坐在這兒
什麼也不做了。 」
蟾蜍坐在那兒，
什麼事也不做。
青蛙陪著他。

坐了老半天， 青蛙說：
「 蟾蜍， 天快黑了，
我們現在該回去
睡覺了。 」

16

「睡覺！」蟾蜍大聲喊起來：

「對啦，那是我工作表上

最後一條啦！」

蟾蜍撿起一根樹枝

在地上寫著：

睡覺

然後畫掉了：

~~睡覺~~

「好啦，」蟾蜍說：

「我全天的工作

全畫掉了！」

青蛙說：

「我真高興。」

於是青蛙和蟾蜍

立刻睡著了。

花　園

青蛙在他的花園裡工作。
蟾蜍走過來說：
「青蛙，你這花園
真漂亮啊。」
「是啊，」青蛙說：
「這花園漂亮是漂亮，
可也滿累人的。」
蟾蜍說：
「我也希望有個花園呢。」
青蛙伸手拿出一點東西，
他說：
「這是一些花兒的種子，
把它們種在地裡，
不久你就會有一個
花園了。」

18

「要多久？」蟾蜍問。

「很快。」青蛙說。

19

蟾蜍跑回家去。
他把花兒種子種在地裡。
蟾蜍對種子說：
「種子種子長出來。」
他走來走去，
走了好幾次，
種子沒有長出來。

20

蟾蜍把他的頭貼近地面，
大聲的說：
「 種子種子長出來！ 」
蟾蜍再看看地上，
種子沒有長出來。

蟾蜍又把他的頭
很近很近的貼近地面，
大聲的喊叫：
「種子種子長出來！」
青蛙從小徑那邊跑過來，
他問：
「剛剛是什麼怪聲音啊？」
蟾蜍說：「我的種子
不肯長出來。」
「是你喊叫的聲音
太大了，」青蛙說：
「這些可憐的種子被你
嚇得不敢長出來。」
「我的種子不敢長？」

22

蟾蜍問。

「當然啦，」青蛙說：
「這幾天你別理它們。
讓陽光照著它們，
讓雨水淋著它們，
不久，你的種子
就會長了。」

23

當天晚上，
蟾蜍從窗戶往外看。
「見鬼！」蟾蜍說：
「我的種子還是沒長嘛，
它們一定是怕黑
才不長的。」
蟾蜍點了幾根蠟燭
走到花園裡去，他說：
「我來給種子
念個故事吧，
這樣它們
就不會害怕了。」
蟾蜍念了一個
好長的故事
給他的種子聽。

24

第二天，
蟾蜍唱了
一整天的歌兒
給他的
種子聽。

第三天，
蟾蜍念了
一整天的小詩
給他的
種子聽。

第四天，
蟾蜍演奏了
一整天的音樂
給他的
種子聽。

蟾蜍低頭看看地上，
種子還是沒有長出來。
「到底我該怎麼辦？」
蟾蜍叫著：
「這些種子一定是
全世界最膽小的種子！」

蟾蜍說完，覺得好累，
不知不覺就睡著了。

27

「蟾蜍，蟾蜍，你醒一一醒，」
青蛙叫他：
「快來看你的花園兒！」
蟾蜍醒來，往花園一一瞧，
好多小小的綠綠的嫩芽
從土裡冒出來了。

28

蟾蜍大叫：「成功了，
我的種子終於不再害怕，
他們長出來了！」
青蛙説：「現在你也快要
有個美麗的花園了。」
「是啊，」蟾蜍説：
「不過，青蛙，
你説得對，弄個花園
確實是非常累人的。」

餅 乾

蟾蜍烤了一些餅乾。

「這些餅乾聞起來真香，」蟾蜍說。

他吃了一塊。

「嗯，吃起來更可口。」他說。

蟾蜍跑到青蛙家。

「青蛙，青蛙，」他大聲的叫：

「快來嚐嚐我做的餅乾。」

青蛙吃了一塊，說：

「我從來沒吃過這麼好吃的餅乾。」

青蛙和蟾蜍
一塊接一塊的
吃了好多餅乾。
青蛙嘴裡塞滿了餅乾，說：
「我說，蟾蜍，
我們不能再吃了，
再吃會吃出病來的。」

「你說得對，」蟾蜍說：
「我們來吃最後的一塊，
就不再吃好啦。」
青蛙和蟾蜍吃了
最後的一塊，
碗裡還剩下很多餅乾。
蟾蜍說：「青蛙，我們
來吃真正最後的一塊，
就不再多吃好啦。」
青蛙和蟾蜍各自吃了
真正最後的一塊餅乾。
「我們一定不要
再吃了！」

33

蟾蜍一面說，
一面又吃了一塊。
「對！」青蛙一面說，
一面伸手又抓了一塊。
「我們需要有意志力。」
「什麼是意志力？」
蟾蜍問。

34

「意志力就是你忍著，
不去做你很想做的
那件事。」青蛙說。
「是不是就像我們
忍著不去吃掉
這裡所有的餅乾那樣？」
蟾蜍問。
「對了。」青蛙說。

35

青蛙把剩下的餅乾
放在一個盒子裡。

「好了，」他說：

「這樣一來，我們就
不會再吃餅乾了。」

「可是我們可以
把盒子打開啊。」
蟾蜍說。

「說的也是。」青蛙說。

36

青蛙用細繩子
把餅乾盒子綁起來。
「好了，」 他說：
「這樣一來， 我們就
不會再吃餅乾了。」
蟾蜍說：
「可是我們可以
把繩子剪斷，
把盒子打開啊。」
「說的也是。」 青蛙說。

青蛙找來一個梯子。
他把餅乾盒子
放在高高的架子上。

38

「好了，」青蛙說：

「這樣一來，我們就

不會再吃餅乾了。」

蟾蜍說：

「可是我們可以

爬上梯子，

把餅乾盒子

從架子上拿下來，

剪斷繩子，

打開盒子啊。」

「說的也是。」青蛙說。

青蛙爬上梯子，

從架子上把盒子拿下來，

剪斷了繩子，

打開了盒子。

39

青蛙把這個盒子
拿到屋外，
他大聲的叫著：
「嗨！鳥兒們，
來吃餅乾！」
鳥兒們從四面八方飛來。
他們把所有的餅乾
都叼走了。
「這樣一來，
我們再也沒有餅乾吃了，」
蟾蜍難過的說：
「一片都沒
得吃了。」

「不錯，」青蛙說：
「可是我們有
很多很多的意志力啊。」
「青蛙，你留著
你的意志力吧！」
蟾蜍說：
「我這就回家去，
烤它一個蛋糕來吃。」

惡龍與巨人

青蛙和蟾蜍
同看一本書。
蟾蜍說：
「這本書裡的人物
好勇敢喔。
他們又打惡龍
又打巨人的，
一點也不怕。」
青蛙說：
「不知道我們倆
勇敢不勇敢。」
青蛙和蟾蜍一起站在
鏡子前面往裡瞧。

「我們看起來是
挺勇敢的嘛。」青蛙說。
「是啊，可是我們真的
勇敢嗎？」蟾蜍問。

43

青蛙和蟾蜍到外面去。

青蛙說：

「我們來爬這座山試試，

看我們到底勇敢不勇敢。」

青蛙一路跳過石頭

往上爬，

蟾蜍喘著氣跟在他後頭。

他們來到一個

黑漆漆的洞口，

44

一條大蛇從洞裡爬出來。
這條大蛇看見了
青蛙和蟾蜍， 他說：
「 你們好啊， 我的午餐！ 」
說著， 他就張開了大嘴。
青蛙和蟾蜍跳著逃開了。
蟾蜍渾身發抖。
「 我不怕！ 」
他大聲的說。

他們爬到
更高一點的地方，
聽到一陣轟隆隆的巨響。
好多大石頭
從山上滾下來。

「山崩了！」蟾蜍大叫。

46

青蛙和蟾蜍跳著逃開了。
青蛙全身直打哆嗦。
「我不怕！」
他大聲的說。

47

他們爬到了山頂。
一隻老鷹的影子
從他們的頭上罩下來。
青蛙和蟾蜍跳到一塊
大石頭底下躲著。
老鷹飛走了。

48

「我們不怕！」

青蛙和蟾蜍

同時尖聲的叫。

然後，

他們飛快的跑下山去。

他們跑過

發現山崩的地方，

他們跑過

看見大蛇的地方，

他們一口氣

跑到蟾蜍的家。

蟾蜍说：
「青蛙，我真高興有
你這麼一個勇敢的朋友。」
說完，他跳上床，
拉起被子，
把頭蒙起來。
青蛙說：「蟾蜍，
我也很高興認識
你這樣勇敢的伙伴。」
說完，他跳進了衣櫥，
關上櫥門。
蟾蜍躲在床上，
青蛙藏在衣櫥裡。
他們待了好久好久，
一起感受那勇敢的滋味。

50

夢

蟾蜍睡著了，
他做了一個夢。
夢見他站在舞臺上，
穿著表演的服裝。
蟾蜍看了看漆黑的臺下。
他看見青蛙坐在戲院裡。
遠處傳來一個陌生的
聲音說：
「現在介紹全世界
最偉大的蟾蜍先生出場！」

蟾蜍深深一鞠躬。

青蛙在下面歡呼：

「蟾蜍萬歲！」

這時，他好像變小了。

那陌生的聲音說：

「現在請蟾蜍先生

彈奏鋼琴，

他彈得非常美妙。」

54

蟾蜍就彈起鋼琴來，
一個音符都沒彈錯。
蟾蜍得意的大聲說：
「青蛙， 你能夠
彈得這麼好嗎？ 」
「不能， 」 青蛙說。
在蟾蜍的眼裡，
青蛙變得更小了。

55

那陌生的聲音宣布：
「現在蟾蜍先生要表演
高空走鋼索，
他是絕對不會掉下來的。」

56

蟾蜍就在高空走著鋼索。
他得意的說：
「青蛙， 你會表演
這種特技嗎？」

「不會。」
青蛙悄聲的說。
他顯得很小、 很小。

那陌生的聲音又宣布：
「現在蟾蜍先生
要表演跳舞，
他的舞跳得非常的棒。」

58

蟾蜍一面在舞臺上
滿場飛舞， 一面問：
「青蛙， 你能跳得
這麼棒嗎？」
沒有回答。
蟾蜍往臺下瞧，
青蛙變得太小了，
小得誰也看不見他，
誰也聽不到他。
「青蛙，」 蟾蜍說：
「你在哪兒啊？」
還是沒有回答。
「青蛙，
我做錯了
什麼事嗎？」
蟾蜍叫著。

接著又傳來

那陌生的聲音：

「現在最偉大的

蟾蜍先生要……」

「閉嘴！」蟾蜍一聲尖叫：

「青蛙，青蛙，

你到哪裡去了？」

蟾蜍在一片黑暗中

不停的打轉兒。

「青蛙，求你回來吧，」

60

他大聲說：
「你不在，
我好孤單啊！」

61

「我在這兒哪，」
青蛙說。

青蛙站在蟾蜍的床邊，
他說：

「蟾蜍，醒一醒。」

「青蛙，真的是你嗎？」
蟾蜍問。

「當然是我嘍。」

62

蟾蜍又問：
「你還是原來那麼大嗎？」
「是啊，我想是吧。」
青蛙說。
蟾蜍看到外面的陽光
穿過窗戶射進屋子裡，
他說：「青蛙，
我真高興你來了。」
「不來才怪！」青蛙說。

63

然後青蛙和蟾蜍
吃了一頓豐盛的早餐。
吃過早餐，
他們兩個快快樂樂
共同度過了漫長的一天。

64

A list

One morning Toad sat in bed.

"I have many things to do," he said.

"I will write them all down on a list

so that I can remember them."

Toad wrote on a piece of paper:

A List of things to do today

Then he wrote:

Wake up

"I have done that," said Toad,

and he crossed out:

~~Wake up~~

Then Toad wrote other things

on the paper.

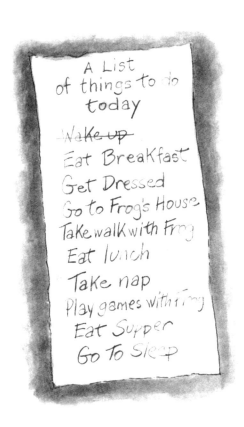

A List
of things to do
today

Wake up
Eat Breakfast
Get Dressed
Go to Frog's House
Take walk with Frog
Eat lunch
Take nap
Play games with Frog
Eat Supper
Go To Sleep

"There," said Toad.
"Now my day is all written down."
He got out of bed and had something to eat.
Then Toad crossed out:

Eat Breakfast

66

Toad took his clothes out of the closet
and put them on.
Then he crossed out:
~~Get Dressed~~
Toad put the list on his pocket.

He opened the door
and walked out into the morning.
Soon Toad was at Frog's front door.
He took the list from his pocket
and crossed out:
~~Go to Frog's House~~

Toad knocked at the door.
"Hello," said Frog.
"Look at my list of things to do," said Toad.
"Oh," said Frog, "that is very nice."
Toad said, "My list tells me that
we will go for a walk."
"All right," said Frog. "I am ready."

Frog and Toad went on a long walk.
Then Toad took the list
from his pocket again.
He crossed out:

~~Take walk with Frog~~

Just then there was a strong wind.
It blew the list out of Toad's hand.
The list blew high up into the air.
"Help!" cried Toad.
"My list is blowing away.

What will I do without my list?"

"Hurry!" said Frog.
"We will run and catch it."
"No!" shouted Toad.
"I cannot do that."
"Why not?" asked Frog.
"Because," wailed Toad,
"running after my list is not

one of the things that I wrote
on my list of things to do!"

Frog ran after the list.
He ran over hills and swamps,
but the list blew on and on.
At last Frog came back to Toad.
"I am sorry," gasped Frog,
"but I could not catch your list."
"Blah," said Toad.

"I cannot remember any of the things
that were on my list of things to do.
I will just have to sit here and do nothing,"
said Toad.
Toad sat and did nothing.
Frog sat with him.
After a long time Frog said,
"Toad, it is getting dark.
We should be going to sleep now."

"Go to sleep!" shouted Toad.

"That was the last thing on my list!"

Toad wrote on the ground with a stick:

Go to sleep

Then he crossed out :

~~Go to sleep~~

"There," said Toad.

"Now my day is all crossed out!"

"I am glad," said Frog.

Then Frog and Toad went right to sleep.

The Garden

Frog was in his garden.

Toad came walking by.

"What a fine garden you have, Frog," he said.

"Yes," said Frog. "It is very nice,

but it was hard work."

"I wish I had a garden," said Toad.

"Here are some flower seeds.

Plant them in the ground," said Frog,

"and soon you will have a garden."

"How soon?" asked Toad.

"Quite soon," said Frog.

Toad ran home.

He planted the flower seeds.

"Now seeds," said Toad, "start growing."

Toad walked up and down a few times.

The seeds did not start to grow.

Toad put his head close to the ground
and said loudly,
"Now seeds, start growing!"
Toad looked at the ground again.
The seeds did not start to grow.

Toad put his head very close to the ground
and shouted,
"NOW SEEDS,
START GROWING!"
Frog came running up the path.
"What is all this noise?" he asked.
"My seeds will not grow," said Toad.
"You are shouting too much," said Frog.
"These poor seeds are afraid to grow."
"My seeds are afraid to grow?"

asked Toad.
"Of course," said Frog.
"Leave them alone for a few days.
Let the sun shine on them,

let the rain fall on them.
Soon your seeds will start to grow."

That night Toad looked out of his window.
"Drat!" said Toad.
"My seed have not started to grow.
They must be afraid of the dark."
Toad went out to his garden
with some candles.
"I will read the seeds a story," said Toad.
"Then they will not be afraid."
Toad read a long story to his seeds.

All the next day
Toad sang songs to his seeds.
And all the next day
Toad read poems to his seeds.
And all the next day
Toad played music for his seeds.

73

Toad looked at the ground.

The seeds still did not start to grow.

"What shall I do?" cried Toad.

"These must be the most frightened seeds

in the whole world!"

Then Toad felt very tired,

and he fell asleep.

"Toad, Toad, wake up," said Frog.

"Look at your garden!"

Toad looked at his garden.

Little green plants were coming up

out of the ground.

"At last," shouted Toad,

"my seeds have stopped being afraid

to grow!"

"And now you will have

a nice garden too," said Frog.

"Yes," said Toad, "but you were right,

Frog. It was very hard wrok."

74

Cookies

Toad baked some cookies.
"These cookies smell very good,"
 said Toad.
He ate one.
"And they taste even better," he said.
Toad ran to Frog's house.
"Frog, Frog," cried Toad,
"taste these cookies that I have made."
Frog ate one of the cookies.
"These are the best cookies
I have ever eaten!" said Frog.

Frog and Toad ate many cookies,
one after another.
"You know, Toad," said Frog,
with his mouth full,
"I think we should stop eating.
We will soon be sick."

"You are right," said Toad.

"Let us eat one last cookie,

and then we will stop."

Frog and Toad ate one last cookie.

There were many cookies left in the bowl.

"Frog," said Toad,

"let us eat one very last cookie,

and then we will stop."

Frog and Toad ate one very last cookie.

"We must stop eating!"

cried Toad as he ate another.

"Yes," said Frog, reaching for a cookie,

"we need will power."

"What is will power?" asked Toad.

"Will power is trying hard

not to do something

that you really want to do," said Frog.

"You mean like trying *not* to eat

all of these cookies?" asked Toad.

76

"Right," said Frog.

Frog put the cookies in a box.
"There," he said.
"Now we will not eat any more cookies."
"But we can open the box," said Toad.
"That is true," said Frog.

Frog tied some string around the box.
"There," he said.
"Now we will not eat any more cookies."
"But we can cut the string
and open the box," said Toad.
"That is true," said Frog.

Frog got a ladder.
He put the box up on a high shelf.

"There," said Frog.
"Now we will not eat any more cookies."

"But we can climb the ladder
and take the box down from the shelf
and cut the string and open the box,"
said Toad.
"That is true," said Frog.
Frog climbed the ladder
and took the box down from the shelf.
He cut the string and opened the box.

Frog took the box outside.
He shouted in a loud voice,
"HEY BIRDS,
HERE ARE COOKIES!"
Birds came from everywhere.
They picked up all the cookies
in their beaks and flew away.
"Now we have no more cookies to eat,"
said Toad sadly.
"Not even one."

"Yes," said Frog, "but we have lots
and lots of will power."
"You may keep it all, Frog,"
said Toad.
"I am going home now
to bake a cake."

Dragons and Giants

Frog and Toad were reading a book
together.
"The people in this book are brave,"
said Toad.
"They fight dragons and giants,
and they are never afraid."
"I wonder if we are brave," said Frog.
Frog and Toad looked into a mirror.

"We look brave," said Frog.
"Yes, but are we?" asked Toad.

Frog and Toad went outside.
"We can try to climb this mountain,"
said Frog. "That should tell us
if we are brave."
Frog went leaping over rocks,
and Toad came puffing up behind him.

They came to a dark cave.

A big snake came out of the cave.
"Hello lunch," said the snake
when he saw Frog and Toad.
He opened his wide mouth.
Frog and Toad jumped away.
Toad was shaking.
"I am not afraid!" he cried.

They climbed higher,
and they heard a loud noise.
Many large stones
were rolling down the mountain.
"It's an avalanche!" cried Toad.

Frog and Toad jumped away.
Frog was trembling.
"I am not afraid!" he shouted.

They came to the top of the mountain.
The shadow of a hawk fell over them.
Frog and Toad jumped under a rock.
The hawk flew away.

"We are not afraid!"
screamed Frog and Toad at the same time.
Then they ran down the mountain
very fast.
They ran past the place
where they saw the avalanche.
They ran past the place
where they saw the snake.
They ran all the way to Toad's house.

"Frog, I am glad to have a brave friend
like you," said Toad.
He jump into the bed
and pulled the covers over his head.
"And I am happy to know a brave person
like you, Toad," said Frog.

82

He jumped into the closet
and shut the door.
Toad stayed in the bed,
and Frog stayed in the closet.
They stayed there for a long time,
just feeling very brave together.

The Dream

Toad was asleep,

and he was having a dream.

He was on a stage,

and he was wearing a costume.

Toad looked out into the dark.

Frog was sitting in the theater.

A strange voice from far away said,

"PRESENTING THE GREATEST TOAD

IN ALL THE WORLD!"

Toad took a deep bow.

Frog looked smaller as he shouted,

"Hooray for Toad!"

"TOAD WILL NOW PLAY THE PIANO

VERY WELL," said the strange voice.

Toad played the piano,

and he did not miss a note.

84

"Frog," cried Toad,
"can you play the piano like this?"
"No," said Frog.
It seemed to Toad that
Frog looked even smaller.

"TOAD WILL NOW WALK
ON A HIGH WIRE,
AND HE WILL NOT FALL DOWN,"
said the voice.

Toad walked on the high wire.
"Frog," cried Toad,
"can you do tricks like this ?"
"No," peeped Frog,
who looked very, very small.

"TOAD WILL NOW DANCE,
AND HE WILL BE WONDERFUL,"
said the voice.

85

"Frog, can you be as wonderful as this?"
said Toad as he danced all over the stage.
There was no answer.
Toad looked out into the theater.
Frog was so small that he could not
be seen or heard.
"Frog," said Toad, "where are you?"
There was still no answer.
"Frog, what have I done?" cried Toad.

Then the voice said,
"THE GREATEST TOAD WILL NOW..."
"Shut up!" screamed Toad.
"Frog, Frog, where have you gone?"
Toad was spinning in the dark.
"Come back, Frog,"

he shouted.
"I will be lonely!"

"I am right here," said Frog.

Frog was standing near Toad's bed.

"Wake up, Toad," he said.

"Frog, is that really you?" said Toad.

"Of course it is me," said Frog.

"And are you your own right size?"
asked Toad.

"Yes, I think so," and Frog.

Toad looked at the sunshine coming
through the window.

"Frog," he said,

"I am so glad that you came over."

"I always do," said Frog.

Then Frog and Toad ate a big breakfast.

And after that
they spent a fine, long day together.